What's for Lunch, Charley?

By MARGARET HODGES

Pictures by ALIKI

SCHOLASTIC **SBS** BOOK SERVICES

Published by Scholastic Book Services, a division
of Scholastic Magazines, Inc., New York, N. Y.

For Fletcher

Copyright © 1961 by Margaret Hodges. This edition is published by Scholastic Book Services, a division of Scholastic Magazines, Inc., by arrangement with The Dial Press.

4th printing . . . . February 1967

Printed in the U.S.A.

Contents

Charley's Hard Life

HURRY, Charley, hurry!" Charley's mother was calling from the kitchen. She was packing his lunch box.

Charley Rivers always had to hurry to be on time for school. First he had to wake up, get up, and wash. Then he had to find his clothes and put them on. He had to eat breakfast. In winter he had to put on his coat, cap, galoshes, and gloves. Last of all he had to remember to take his schoolbooks and his homework. And his lunch box.

Somehow, Charley's lunch box was the hardest thing to remember every morning.

"Hurry, hurry, hurry. That's all I do every morning," said Charley, when he was eating breakfast and still hurrying.

"Why?" said his father. "You get up at seven o'clock. That gives you two hours to get to school only four blocks away."

"I know," said Charley. "Now you're going to tell me that in the army I'd have to get up at *five* o'clock."

"That's right," his father said.

"And you're going to tell me that you walked four *miles* to school when you were my age," added Charley.

"At *least* four miles," his father said. "Maybe more. On country roads. And I was always on time."

"Always?" asked Charley's mother, buttering toast.

"Well, nearly always," his father said. He finished his coffee and stood up. "Don't forget your lunch box."

"I won't," said Charley.

And that morning he didn't forget his lunch box.

Everything had gone well so far that morning. When a day starts out well, it usually goes on well. When it starts out badly, everything usually goes wrong all day. Charley had noticed that.

This morning was good. He had gotten up soon after the alarm clock rang. He hadn't stayed in the bathroom too long making faces at himself in the mirror. For once he had put his clean clothes on a chair the night before, just the way his mother had told him to do. Breakfast tasted good. His coat and cap were on the hook, right where he had left them. Galoshes underneath. Gloves in his pocket. His homework was all done. Schoolbooks were piled neatly in the front hall. And he remembered to get his lunch box from the kitchen table.

"What's for lunch?" he asked his mother.

"Same as usual," his mother said. "Sandwich, milk, fruit, and cookie."

"Again?" said Charley.

His father came into the kitchen to kiss Charley's mother good-by.

"If you don't like it, go and eat at the King Charles," said Charley's father, looking at the lunch box.

Charley laughed. He thought his father was a very funny man. So did Charley's mother.

The King Charles was a big hotel that Charley passed every morning on his way to school. A man in a wonderful uniform stood in front of the King Charles to open the door for people. It was like a palace.

That was why Charley's family had a family joke. When the dishes had to be washed, or when you didn't like your dinner, someone was sure to say, "If you don't like it, go and eat at the King Charles." Then the whole family would laugh.

Charley wasn't really complaining about his lunch. He always liked what his mother put in his lunch box. Besides, he knew that his mother had to hurry in the morning even faster than he had to hurry. She was a schoolteacher. Every morning she packed a lunch box for herself just like Charley's lunch box. Then she hurried off to her school, while Charley hurried off to his.

Charley picked up his lunch box and tucked his schoolbooks under his arm on his way out of the front door. He started down the street toward school.

Charley Meets a King

WHEN Charley came to the end of his block and crossed the street, there was the King Charles Hotel. It had several fancy shops in front.

There was the Bandbox, a shop selling ladies' dresses. Charley never looked at them much.

Next came a shop that sold ties and belts and handkerchiefs for men. "The Gentry — Gentlemen's Outfitters," the window said. Sometimes Charley looked in that window. He wondered if he would ever want to wear the sort of clothes he saw in there. He thought maybe he would. His father had some nice ties. His father always looked just right, Charley thought. He would like to look just like his father when he grew up.

After the men's shop came the King Charles Candy Shop. Charley always stopped to look in that window. There were big boxes of candy on lace-paper mats. Some were closed and tied up in ribbon bows. Some were open, full of chocolates and bonbons in wonderful shapes and colors. Charley's mouth watered when he looked at them.

After the candy shop came the main front door of the King Charles Hotel. There was a green-and-white striped canopy. There were red wooden tubs with little trees growing in them. And there was a doorman.

The doorman's name was Mr. King. At least Charley thought so.

Charley had never had enough nerve to speak to him. But the doorman looked as if he must be the King part of the King Charles Hotel.

He was over six feet tall, even taller than Charley's father. He wore a dark-blue cap with a visor, like a general in the army. He wore a long blue overcoat with bright gold buttons, and his trousers had a gold stripe down the side. He always wore a pair of clean white gloves.

Mr. King stood right in front of the front door. When anyone wanted to go in or out, Mr. King

opened the front door and saluted. Charley admired him very much.

After the front door there were more shops, and then Charley came to another street. There was a traffic light at that corner. All the children going to school waited for the light to change to green. Then they went on to school together.

When Charley was on time for school, the last two blocks were great. All of his friends were going toward school at the same time. Charley walked with his best friend, Wally Williams. And sometimes he walked with Jane Lane. He liked Jane a lot, too. Right now he was planning to send her a valentine. In those last two blocks on the way to school, everybody laughed and talked and had fun.

But when Charley was late, he had to run the whole way, and the last two blocks felt very lonely.

This morning, though, was a good morning. There were fur coats in the window of the Bandbox. And in the corner of the window was a stuffed beaver. That was very interesting! It was the only really interesting thing that Charley had ever seen in the window of the Bandbox.

The Gentry was showing red ties. In the center of the window was a log with a shining hatchet stuck in it. That was because it would soon be Washington's Birthday.

The King Charles Candy Shop window was the best of all. It was full of big red hearts for Valentine's Day. The boxes were shaped like hearts, and so were some of the pieces of candy. Charley thought he would like to buy a box of candy hearts. He wouldn't mind having the hatchet, too. And the stuffed beaver.

But all that would cost a lot of money. Charley had just a dollar. And he wasn't supposed to spend that dollar unless he really had to. It was a silver dollar. His father had brought it home from a business trip.

The silver dollar was fastened to a clip. The clip was meant to hold paper dollars, but Charley didn't have any paper dollars. He carried the silver dollar in his pocket, where it jingled against his pennies, nickels, and dimes. It was always good for a joke.

He could say, "I'm down to my last dollar." Then he could show it to someone who hadn't seen it before. People were always interested in seeing a silver dollar.

When Charley reached the front door of the King Charles Hotel, Mr. King was just coming out to begin his day's work. The visor of his cap was polished like a mirror, and his white gloves were spotless. When he saw Charley, he nodded.

Charley was so surprised that he dropped his arithmetic book. His homework started to blow away down the sidewalk.

Mr. King reached down and picked it up before it could blow into the street. Then he picked up the book, slipped the paper neatly inside, and handed it to Charley.

"There you are," he said. "You've got your

hands pretty full, haven't you?"

"Yes," said Charley. He couldn't think of anything else to say. Why did he have to be so dumb the one time he had a chance to talk to Mr. King?

He tucked the arithmetic book under his arm and started on. Then he remembered.

"Thanks," he said. "Thanks a lot, Mr. ——"

"Murphy," said the doorman. "I've been seeing you just about every day. What's your name?"

"Charley Rivers," said Charley.

"Oh, sure," said Mr. Murphy. "Rivers. You must be Mr. Rivers' boy. Mr. Rivers comes here to lunch sometimes."

"Does he?" said Charley. "My father does?"

"Sure thing," said Mr. Murphy. "On business."

"Well!" said Charley. He had never felt so important.

Suddenly he knew that he had been talking to Mr. Murphy for quite a long time. If he didn't hurry, he was going to be late for school.

Rosabelle's Lunch

WHEN Charley got to school that day, there was a new girl. Her name was Rosabelle Ruggles. There was an empty seat right across the aisle from Charley. Miss Gay, Charley's teacher, told Rosabelle to sit there.

Charley thought she was pretty. She was more dressed up than any other girl in the class, much more than plain Jane Lane. Rosabelle's hair was curled all over. Jane's hair was straight. And Rosabelle had shiny pink polish on her fingernails.

Charley had seen plenty of ladies who wore nail polish. But this was the first time he'd ever seen a girl his own age with her fingernails painted.

When noon came, some of the children went home for lunch. Those who stayed had to wash their hands and get their lunch boxes from their lockers. Then they had to go back to their seats and eat. There was no cafeteria in Charley's school.

Miss Gay went to the teachers' room to eat her lunch, and everyone was supposed to be good while she was gone. When lunch was over, you could go to the gym or to the playground to play.

Charley washed his hands. He got his lunch box from his locker and took it back to his seat. He opened the lunch box and took out a paper napkin to spread on his desk. Then he saw Rosabelle coming back to her seat.

"So!" he thought, "she is going to stay for lunch, too." Everybody began eating and talking.

Charley had a sandwich wrapped in wax paper. He unwrapped it and looked at the filling. Peanut butter! His favorite kind. There was an apple in his lunch box, too, and an oatmeal cookie. It was all just as usual — a sandwich and milk, some sort of fruit, and some sort of cookie. All of the others had about the same things in their lunch boxes.

Then Charley looked at Rosabelle. She was spreading out a napkin on her desk, but — it wasn't a paper napkin. It was a real one! A cloth one! What was more, Rosabelle took another real napkin out of her lunch box and spread it on her lap.

Then she took out something wrapped in silver foil. Charley stared. It was a drumstick of fried chicken! Next she unscrewed her thermos bottle and poured out — not milk, but hot tomato soup. Charley could see that it was piping hot.

Rosabelle sat nibbling at the chicken leg and sipping tomato soup. She didn't talk to anybody, because she was new. Charley decided that after lunch he would speak to her.

When Rosabelle had finished the chicken leg and the soup, she took a spoon and a glass jar out of her lunch box. Charley could see what was in the glass jar. Fruit salad! Rosabelle ate all of it.

Charley wondered if there could be anything else in her lunch box. There was. It was a piece of chocolate layer cake with inches of icing. It was wrapped in silver foil, too. Charley had never seen anything that looked more delicious.

Rosabelle finished the cake down to the last crumb. Then she put everything neatly away in her lunch box and carried it out to her locker.

Charley had spent so much time watching Rosabelle that he was the last one to finish lunch. When he went out to the playground, a game of tag was going on. Wally Williams was playing, and so was Jane Lane. She was screaming and running. Her coat was unbuttoned, and her straight hair was whipping around in the wind. It looked like an old mop.

Rosabelle wasn't playing tag. She was sitting in a swing, but she wasn't even swinging. She didn't look lonely. In fact, she looked perfectly satisfied. Her coat was buttoned up neatly. Every curl was in place. She was looking at her fingernails.

Now was the time for Charley to speak to Rosabelle. But he didn't. He started to play tag. Jane Lane was "it." Before he knew what had happened, Jane had tagged him.

"Got you!" she screamed. "I got Charley Rivers!" And she raced off.

When the bell rang at the end of the lunch

hour, Charley still hadn't spoken to Rosabelle.

During the afternoon Miss Gay called on Rosabelle once or twice. But all she said was "Yes" or "No" or "I don't know." She wasn't a bit like Jane Lane, who always had something to say for herself.

Charley finally thought of something to say to Rosabelle. When school was over, everybody went to the lockers out in the hall. Charley saw Rosabelle standing by her locker, putting on her coat.

"See you tomorrow," he said.

Rosabelle didn't say anything, but she smiled. She had a dimple.

A Valentine for Someone

WHAT did you think of her?" asked Wally Williams. They were on the way home from school, waiting at the corner for the stop light to change to green.

Charley didn't ask whom Wally meant. He knew.

"All right, I guess," he said.

"I thought so too," Wally said. "Well, see you tomorrow."

"See you," said Charley. The light changed to green, and he crossed the street.

There was Mr. Murphy still on duty in front of the King Charles. Mr. Murphy was rocking back and forth from toe to heel, heel to toe. Charley guessed that his feet must be tired. Still, Mr. Murphy stood up straight. That was part of his job. When he saw Charley, he smiled.

"Have a good day?" he asked.

"Pretty good," said Charley. "Did you?"

"About the same as usual," said Mr. Murphy.

Charley would have liked to stop and talk to him, but he thought it probably wasn't part of Mr. Murphy's job to stand there talking. Especially to someone who was just passing by.

"See you tomorrow," he said.

Mr. Murphy smiled and saluted, just as if Charley had been a grown-up person going into the King Charles Hotel. He was certainly a nice, friendly man.

If Mr. Murphy hadn't been such a nice, friendly man, Charley wouldn't have done what he did next. He decided to buy some candy in the King Charles Candy Shop.

Charley usually went to the corner drugstore

to buy his candy. At the corner drugstore, he could buy a good chocolate bar for five cents. But today he was in the mood for something different. The candy shop, like everything else at the King Charles Hotel, was fancy — just what Charley wanted today.

As he opened the door, a wonderful puff of warm air met him. It smelled of chocolate. All of the glass cases were full of chocolates and bonbons, and everywhere Charley looked he saw bright-red boxes.

There was a lady behind the counter. She was wearing a blue dress and a frilly white apron. She was humming a tune while she filled a big heart-shaped box with candy. She looked up when Charley came in.

Charley wouldn't have been surprised if the lady had told him to go away. The candy shop looked as if it were meant only for grown-up people. But the lady behind the counter said, "May I help you?"

"Yes," said Charley. "I'd like to buy some candy for a valentine."

The lady nodded and asked, "How much would you like to spend?"

Charley put his books and his lunch box on the floor. Then he reached into his pocket and brought out everything that was there. He put on the counter his silver-dollar money clip, one quarter, one dime, two nickels, and eight pennies. Also two bottle tops from pop bottles. (Charley had a collection of these at home.) Sticking to one of the bottle tops was a French stamp that his father had torn from a letter. (Charley was interested in stamps.)

He looked at the pile of coins and other things on the counter.

"What could I get for a quarter?" he asked.

"H'm," said the lady. "Let me see. I think we have something for a quarter."

She slid open the door at the back of the glass case and brought out a little heart-shaped box. It

was so small that it fitted the palm of her hand. But it was very, very nice. In it was one chocolate candy heart.

"I'll take it," said Charley. He held out his hand.

"Wait just a minute," said the lady. She put the red top on the box. Then she put the whole thing into a small, square cardboard box. There was a big roll of shiny white wrapping paper behind the counter. All over the paper in gold letters were printed gold crowns and the words *King Charles*.

The lady tore off a neat strip of the paper and wrapped Charley's box, folding every corner sharply and squarely. Then she tied the box in bright-red ribbon. Her hands flashed like magic while she made a pompom bow for the top of the box.

"There you are," said the lady. She slipped the beautiful package into a white paper bag and handed it to Charley with a smile. He gave her the quarter.

"Thank you," said Charley. He scooped up the rest of his coins and the bottle tops, and put them back into his pocket.

"Thank *you*," said the lady. "Come in again."

Charley picked up his books and his lunch box. He had to carry them all under his left arm and in his left hand. His right hand had to be free to carry the King Charles candy, the fanciest thing he had ever bought. It was worth a quarter, any day!

"You've got your hands pretty full there," said the lady. She came around from in back of the counter and pushed open the door for Charley. She was just as nice and friendly as Mr. Murphy.

Man to Man

CHARLEY went out into the cold fresh air, and the door of the candy shop closed behind him. The smell of chocolate was gone. He was still in the mood for something a little different from his usual day.

Now he was in front of The Gentry. The red ties were there in the window, and so was the log with the shining hatchet stuck in it. Charley still thought he would like to have the hatchet. He went into the men's shop. He would never have done it if the lady in the candy shop hadn't been so nice.

The men's shop smelled different from the candy shop, but it was even more exciting. There was a smell of leather and wool and shaving cream and tobacco all mixed together. In fact, it smelled like men, and Charley wasn't a man yet. Suddenly he knew that he really didn't belong in this place.

They would surely tell him so. They would say, "Run along home. You don't belong here."

Charley was about to turn and go out again when someone spoke to him.

A young man was folding some sweaters in the back of the shop. He had looked up as Charley came in and now he said, "Hi."

Charley was surprised. He *wasn't* being thrown out of this fancy grown-up shop. And he had thought he might need all his nerve to ask about the hatchet. Now, instead, it was easy.

"I just wanted to ask a question," he said.

"O.K.," said the young man. "Shoot."

"How much is the hatchet?" asked Charley.

The young man stopped folding sweaters. "Hatchet?" he said. "Oh! The one in the window. That's not for sale. That belongs to me. It's my old Boy Scout hatchet."

"Were you a Boy Scout?" Charley asked, more surprised than ever. "I'm a Cub Scout."

"Good for you," said the young man. "Stick with it. Some day you'll be a Boy Scout and then you can save up your money for a hatchet."

"I'd like to get one right now," said Charley.

"Better wait," the young man said. "If you had one now, you'd probably cut your arm off. Better stick to building bird houses for a while."

"How did you know we're building bird houses?" asked Charley.

"Because I remember everything I did when I was a Cub Scout. February is the month for building bird houses. You can build something bigger and better every year. Know what I'm building right now?"

"No," said Charley. "What?"

"I'm building a shack," said the young man. "I'm saving all the money I earn at this job, and I'm going to have a nice little shack where I can hunt and fish. I'll be using that hatchet."

"That sounds great," said Charley. The day was going better and better. This was one of the nicest people he had ever met. He hadn't scared Charley at all. He wasn't what you'd expect in such a fancy place. He had turned out to be just a grown-up Cub Scout. He had to save his money to buy things that he wanted the same way Charley did. And he had talked to Charley as man to man.

Still, Charley didn't want to take up too much of his time. He remembered what his father said: "Go while they still want you to stay." That was the grown-up way to end a visit.

"I've got to be going," he said. "Maybe some time I can come in and buy a tie for my father or something."

"Do that," said the young man. "And keep working on that bird house. Make it a good one. Before you know it, you'll be a Boy Scout and you'll have a hatchet."

Charley looked back and nodded as he went out the door. He felt wonderful. He had made another friend at the King Charles Hotel.

Well, he might try his luck one more time, since everybody at the King Charles was so nice and friendly.

When a day starts out well, it usually goes on well. Charley had one more thing on his mind, now that he had bought a valentine at the candy shop and found out about the hatchet at The Gentry. The beaver! He might as well make a clean sweep and go right on to the ladies' dress shop. This was certainly his day for doing something a little different!

End of a Big Day

WHEN Charley went into the Bandbox, a lady was sitting in a pink chair near the window.

She raised her eyebrows. "Yes?" she said.

Charley thought he was really out of line this time. At the candy shop he had at least bought some candy. In the men's shop he had not bought anything, but he might some day. Here in this shop that smelled of perfume and of ladies, he could never be a customer. He was not going to buy any dresses or fur coats. His galoshes did not belong on these deep, soft carpets.

"You want something?" asked the lady.

Right away Charley knew that she came from another country. He could see that she had to think of the right words to say in English. He knew that he should always be polite to people from other countries.

"Excuse me," he said, very politely and very clearly. "I would like to look at your beaver."

A man came from the back of the shop.

"This little boy likes the beaver," said the lady.

"Ah? He likes little Hugo?" said the man. "Poor Hugo has lost one eye. He has a leg broken. But he helps us to sell fur coats."

Charley looked puzzled.

"Hugo?" he asked.

"Oui, oui, oui, oui," said the man. He reached into the window and brought out the beaver. Tenderly he carried it under his arm and set it on a glass-topped table.

"Hugo. We name him for the greatest writer of France — the greatest writer of the whole world! Victor Hugo!"

"France?" said Charley. "You come from France?"

"Certainly. From France," said the lady. She

leaned forward and her eyes sparkled. "You have been in France maybe?"

ake up?
by ants?
facts
, too.

ve a French
candy on the
le brought out
ith the French

by Dell J. McCormick

ghs, folks think it is
Blue Ox, can drink
d about the popcorn
at stood on its head.
res!

amp," he said.
France, no?"
thought of it
hy not? Today
!
ed the beaver's
refully, he saw

that one eye was missing — the eye that did not show when you looked into the window from the sidewalk. One leg was a little short, too. Victor Hugo had, as the man said, "a leg broken."

"Poor little Hugo," said the lady. "Next week we begin to show spring dresses. We take the fur coats out of the window. Then Hugo must go also."

43

"Where will he go?" asked Charley.

"Who knows?" said the man, patting Hugo's back. "We cannot keep him. He is too old and worn out to be in the window another year. Who would take him?"

"Who would give a home to poor little Hugo?" said the lady.

"I would," said Charley. He was so excited that he could hardly talk. "I'd put him on the bookcase in my bedroom. He'd look great. I've got a collection of a lot of good things on my bookcase. He'd like it there, I'll bet."

"Good," said the man. "You must come next week as soon as you see the spring dresses in the window. Then we give you Hugo."

"I will," said Charley. "Gosh! A real stuffed beaver. I never thought things would turn out like this. I sure have had a big day!"

The lady smiled. Charley patted the beaver's nose and picked up his bottle tops and his candy again.

"Good-by, Victor Hugo," he said. "I'll call you Beavo for short."

He didn't want to leave the Bandbox. He would have liked to play with Victor Hugo, Beavo for short. He liked the friendly French people who had been so kind. Maybe they would say something in French if he stayed long enough.

But again he remembered, "Go while they still want you to stay." He thought he had better not go too far.

"I've got to go," he said. "My mother will be wondering where I am."

"*Au revoir*," said the man. And Charley knew enough to answer, "*Au revoir*."

When he walked out of the Bandbox, he wasn't sure whether he was still walking on deep, soft carpets or walking on air. He had talked to some French people in French. It was almost like taking a trip to France.

What a day it had been! He had really met Mr. Murphy for the first time. Rosabelle had arrived.

And he had gone shopping in three brand-new places that he had never dared to enter before. It was certainly funny how one thing had led to another all day long.

"One thing always does lead to another," his father said that night. Charley had been telling about his good day. "There's just one thing I'd like to know."

"What?" said Charley, climbing into his pajamas.

"Who's going to get that valentine?"

Start of a Bad Day

THE next day started out all wrong for Charley. When the alarm clock rang, it was raining hard. He could hear the rain drumming on the roof, and a cold wind was blowing the curtain. That meant that his mother would want him to wear his gloves and galoshes again.

Charley was so bored with the idea of wearing gloves and galoshes again that he turned over and went back to sleep. The next time he woke up, he heard his mother rattling dishes in the kitchen. "Hurry, Charley, hurry!" she called.

Charley scuttled out of bed and made a bee-line for the bathroom. He locked the door and turned on the water to wash his face. While he waited for the basin to fill, his eye lighted on his father's shaving cream. Charley made some good war-paint stripes with the shaving cream. Then he gripped his toothbrush between his teeth for a scalping knife. He frowned into the mirror.

"Big Chief attack fort," he said.

The wash basin was now full to the brim. If he put his hands in, would it overflow? Not quite. If he put his arms in up to the elbows, would it overflow? The answer was "yes." It crossed his mind that this was an important scientific discovery. His pajama top looked about right for the white coat that a great scientist would wear.

Then he noticed that he was standing in a puddle of water. Charley took a bath towel and mopped up the bathroom floor. His mother's voice came to him from a great distance. "Hurry, Charley, hurry!"

He had better wash his face. He added a little water to the shaving cream on his face and worked up a good beard for a Civil War general. His face looked noble and stern. "Tell them I went down fighting," he said.

Someone was pounding on the bathroom door.

"Great Caesar's ghost!" said his father's voice. "What are you doing in there? Your mother has been calling you for half an hour."

"I'm hurrying as fast as I can!" said Charley.

He plunged his face into the wash basin and blew some bubbles. It must be like this in a submarine. Down, down, down. How long could he stay submerged?

"You've got about five minutes to get out of here," his father called. "Do you want to be late for school?"

"I'm *coming*!" said Charley. With traces of shaving cream still on his face, he unlocked the door and streaked back to his bedroom.

This had to be the day when a shoelace broke. He couldn't find his undershirt, but with any luck his mother might not ask whether he had it on. Over his bare chest he pulled on a white starched shirt with buttons. Last night he had decided to wear one of his best shirts to school today. Now he couldn't remember why. It would really be easier to wear a striped T-shirt the way he usually did. A buttoned shirt was a nuisance, because his mother fussed if it was buttoned up crooked.

He started to take off the white shirt and put on a T-shirt. Then he remembered his reason for wearing the white shirt. Rosabelle! She would be in school again today.

He heard the front door close. That was his father going to work. Now where were his trousers?

"Charley!" his mother called. "You're *awfully* late. I've got to go or I'll be late myself. Eat a good breakfast. Wear your gloves and galoshes. And don't forget your lunch box."

He had already passed the King Charles Hotel when he knew that he had forgotten his lunch box. Well, it was much too late to go back now.

He stood at the corner waiting for the light to change to green. Rain was still coming down, getting his schoolbooks wet. There was a paper sticking out from between the pages of his science book. It was his theme about dinosaurs. It was getting wet, too. He remembered now that he should have checked the spelling on the dinosaur theme and copied the whole thing in ink. He had meant to get up early this morning and do that.

What was Miss Gay going to say? Plenty! This was certainly a terrible day! He wished he could think of someone to blame, but he couldn't think of anyone.

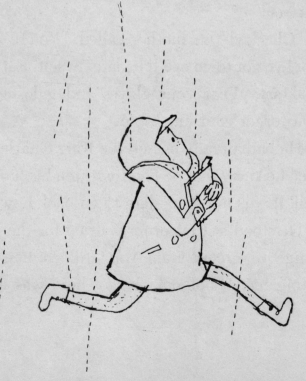

The light changed to green, and Charley splashed across the street. When he reached the other side, he began to run. It was so late that there was no one else on the way to school. The sidewalk was empty and lonely. Long before Charley reached school, he was panting like a race horse, and he was very wet.

In the playground the swings were blowing and clanking against each other in the cold wind. It was the loneliest sound Charley had ever heard.

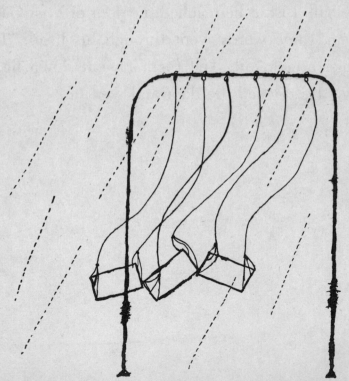

Inside the school everyone else was dry and neat, on time, and hard at work. Outside the school was Charley, all alone, wet and messy, late, his homework unfinished. What would happen to him?

For a minute Charley thought about not going to school at all that day. But all the time his feet kept on going, running through the empty playground.

He went into the school, put his wet things in a heap on the floor of his locker, and ran down the hall. Just as he reached the door of Miss Gay's room, some words went through his head. "Big Chief attack fort. Tell them I went down fighting." He opened the door and went in.

Jane's Lunch

Miss Gay was writing on the blackboard and Wally Williams was standing up to recite. They turned to look at Charley, and so did everyone else in the class.

"Well, Charley, you're very late," said Miss Gay. "What excuse do you have?"

Charley stood there in the doorway, thinking of all the unlucky things that had happened to him ever since he woke up this morning. No one thing had made him late. *Everything* had made him late, but he really had no excuse.

"I couldn't find my clothes," he said.

Luckily, nobody laughed. If they had, Miss

Gay might have sent Charley to the office. Now she said, "Well, Charley, I thought I had heard everything. But that is one excuse I've never heard before today. Take your seat."

Charley took his seat. He was glad to be back where he belonged, and he was glad that Miss Gay hadn't said much about his being late. This day might not turn out to be so bad after all. Rosabelle was sitting across the aisle. She was looking prettier than ever. When Charley sat down, she smiled at him, and he saw the dimple. He was glad he had worn his white starched shirt.

Charley didn't think about his troubles again until science class began. Then he remembered his dinosaur theme. He was going to have to hand it in written in pencil with some words spelled wrong. He would probably get a low mark.

Charley didn't mind getting a low mark in subjects that he didn't know much about. That was only fair. But he *did* know about dinosaurs. He had gone to the library and read every book they had about dinosaurs. It was stupid to get a bad mark just because everything had started out wrong this morning.

He was still feeling gloomy about the dinosaurs when lunch time came. Then he remembered that he didn't have his lunch box.

Miss Gay went to the teachers' room, and everyone else who was staying for lunch went out to the lockers to get lunch boxes. Everyone but Charley. He sat at his desk while the others came back and began to eat.

After a while he opened his desk and got out a large piece of plain paper and a pencil. At the top of the paper he wrote *Custard's Last Stand*. He looked at what he had written. Then he crossed out *Custard's* and wrote *Custer's*.

The smell of food was making him very hungry. He was sure that Wally Williams would have offered him some lunch, but Wally had gone home for lunch today.

Out of the corner of his eye he saw Rosabelle

opening her lunch box. She spread out her real cloth napkin and opened a package wrapped in silver foil. It was a chicken drumstick. Charley wondered if it was the other leg of the same chicken she had eaten yesterday.

She unscrewed the top of her thermos bottle. Tomato soup again, piping hot. The steam smelled wonderful. Rosabelle seemed to have plenty of chicken and plenty of soup. Charley guessed that she had other things in her lunch box, too—maybe fruit salad and chocolate cake.

But Rosabelle didn't offer Charley anything to eat. She sat nibbling the chicken leg and sipping tomato soup.

Charley began to draw a picture. He made General Custer on his horse. Then he made some Indians on horseback with bows and arrows. He drew some soldiers with rifles, falling off their horses.

And all the time, Rosabelle never said a word to Charley.

Then someone was standing in the aisle on the other side of him.

"Aren't you going to eat any lunch?" someone said. Charley looked up. It was Jane Lane.

"I forgot my lunch box," said Charley.

"You can have half of my peanut butter sandwich," Jane said.

"No, thanks," said Charley. If Rosabelle needed all of her big lunch, Jane certainly needed all of her little one.

"How about half of my cookie?" Jane asked.

"No, thanks," said Charley again. And suddenly he added, "I'm going out to lunch."

He put his drawing and his pencil away. Then he walked past Rosabelle and Jane and everybody, out of the room.

Now that he had said it, he had to do it. And there was only one place to go — the King Charles Hotel!

Lunch Like a King

THE wind was still blowing hard, but it had stopped raining. Charley felt better than he had all morning.

Mr. Murphy was standing in front of the main door of the King Charles under the green-and-white canopy. He was stamping his feet on the sidewalk. Charley guessed that his feet must be cold.

"Well, young fellow-me-lad," said Mr. Murphy, "I don't usually see you going by at this time of day."

"I forgot my lunch box," said Charley. "I thought I'd have lunch at the King Charles."

"That's a good idea," said Mr. Murphy. "Do

you have any money with you? It costs something, you know."

"I have some money," Charley said. He reached into his pocket and brought out his silver-dollar money clip. "I'm down to my last dollar. But my father said I could spend it if I ever really had to."

Mr. Murphy looked at the money clip. "Now that's real interesting," he said. "You don't often see a silver dollar."

"Could I use it to buy some lunch?" asked Charley.

"I guess you could," said Mr. Murphy. "Step right this way."

He saluted and opened the big front door for Charley. Then he led the way to a second door marked KING CHARLES DINING ROOM. He opened that door too, and Charley walked in.

The King Charles dining room looked to Charley like the inside of a royal palace. He saw marble columns and deep, soft carpets. There was music in the air. Grown-up people were sitting at tables covered with real cloth tablecloths. Waitresses were moving around in blue dresses and frilly aprons. The room was warm and smelled of good food.

Charley had time to notice all this while he and Mr. Murphy stood inside the doorway. Then he saw a lady coming toward them. She looked rather surprised, but she smiled. Charley noticed that she had a dimple.

"Can I help?" she said to Mr. Murphy.

"You can," said Mr. Murphy. "This is my friend, Charley Rivers. He forgot his lunch box this morning and he's hungry."

He put his hand on Charley's shoulder. "This is Mrs. Ruggles," he said. "She's the new hostess of the King Charles dining room. She'll take care of you."

"What about the bill, Mr. Murphy?" asked Mrs. Ruggles.

Charley looked at her. Her hair was curled all

over. She was plump. And she had pink finger-nails, just like Rosabelle. Rosabelle Ruggles!

"Charley expected to pay for his lunch," said Mr. Murphy. "Just see that he gets all he wants to eat. If he needs credit, call on me. His credit is good with me any time."

"Very well, Mr. Murphy. We'll take care of him," said Mrs. Ruggles.

Mr. Murphy went away, and Mrs. Ruggles helped Charley hang up his coat and cap on a rack at the door. Then she said, "Step right this way."

Charley followed her through the room.

"We're not very crowded this early in the day," said Mrs. Ruggles. "Maybe you'd like a table by the window." She pulled out a chair at a little table by a big plate-glass window, and Charley sat down. Mrs. Ruggles signaled to a waitress. "Luncheon for one," she said. "Mr. Murphy will take care of the bill."

Charley wondered if he were dreaming. The

waitress put a menu on the table in front of him and stood waiting. Charley knew that he was supposed to read the menu and decide quickly what he wanted to eat. But the menu was so big! It was covered with words. There wasn't time to read them. And waitresses do not like to wait.

He could ask for a peanut butter sandwich, an apple, a cookie, and some milk. But that didn't seem like the right thing for lunch at the King Charles.

Charley drew a long breath and said, "Tomato soup, chicken leg, fruit salad, and chocolate cake." Then he added, "Please." He looked up at the waitress, wondering if he had ordered the right things.

She nodded and scribbled something on her order pad. Then she winked at Charley and went away.

Charley was stunned. Everyone was taking care of him. It seemed as if all of his troubles were over forever. He sat up straight like a grown-up person. It was a good thing he had worn his white starched shirt today. He listened to the music. He watched the people going by on the sidewalk outside the big plate-glass window. It was still blowing hard out there. People were clutching their hats and turning up their coat collars as they went by.

In the King Charles dining room Charley sat, warm and comfortable, waiting for his lunch to come. He had a real cloth tablecloth all his own. He had two forks, two knives, and three spoons— all different sizes and shapes. It would be fun to draw a picture on the tablecloth with the edge of a spoon. But he remembered what his mother and father said when he did that at home. He unfolded his napkin, spread it on his lap, and waited.

After a while the waitress came back. She put in front of him a cup of tomato soup, piping hot. She put a basket of crackers and rolls on the table, and added a dish of celery and olives and a butter plate with butter on it.

"That must be for someone else," said Charley. "I didn't order that."

"Don't worry. It comes with the lunch," said the waitress.

She went away again and Charley picked up the cup. He drank all of the soup. Then he ate a buttered roll and some crackers. He finished most of the celery and all of the olives before the waitress came back.

This time she took away his soup cup and put in front of him a large plate. It was almost covered with half of a fried chicken, all in one big piece. There were mashed potatoes on the plate, too, as well as peas and cranberry sauce. On another plate at the side was a big fruit salad.

"You might need some help with this chicken," said Charley's waitress. "It's rather hard to tackle with a knife and fork."

Quickly, easily, she cut off the drumstick for him. "There," she said, "you can start with that. When you're ready for dessert, just let me know.

My name's Nancy." She went away.

Charley wasn't sure whether his mother and father would think he should eat a chicken leg in his fingers at the King Charles. But Nancy seemed to think it was all right. He decided not to worry. He finished the chicken leg and began to eat the fruit salad. When he had eaten half of it, he stopped. He could not eat another bite. He was full to the chin.

There was still a lot of food left on his plate. At home he was always told, "Eat what is put before you." And at home you always could. But who could eat all of this? Well, maybe one person could — Rosabelle. Charley couldn't. He saw Nancy coming.

"Want something?" she said.

Charley shook his head. "I can't finish what I've got," he said.

"Oh, that's too bad," said Nancy. "What about your piece of chocolate cake for dessert?"

Charley didn't even want to think about chocolate cake right now. He shook his head again. "I've got to hurry," he said. "I'll be late for school."

"I'll tell you what," said Nancy. "I'll have them wrap up the cake for you in the kitchen. You can take it along with you. I'll be right back. Here's your bill."

She put the bill face down on the table and went off toward the kitchen.

Charley turned the bill over and looked at it. He couldn't read Nancy's scribbles very well, but he could read what his lunch had cost—three dollars plus tax. Three dollars for one lunch at the King Charles! Charley's stomach turned cold.

The Price of Lunch

WHAT would Mr. Murphy say about such a big bill? And how long would it take Charley to pay him back? He had heard of people who had to wash dishes to pay for the food they had eaten. Charley would be washing dishes at the King Charles for the rest of his life to pay this bill!

Suddenly he remembered that he owed more than three dollars plus tax. He ought to give Nancy a tip. He reached into his pocket and put all of his money on the table, including the silver-dollar money clip. Nancy was coming back. She had wrapped Charley's chocolate cake in silver foil.

"There you are," she said. "It's an end piece covered with icing."

"Thanks," said Charley. "I'll take good care of it." Then he added, "This is for you. I hope it's enough." She had been so nice. You really couldn't pay people for being nice. But he could try. He could give her everything he had.

Nancy looked at Charley's money: one dime, two nickels, eight pennies — and the silver-dollar money clip.

She picked up the clip. "You didn't mean to leave this, did you?" she asked.

"Yes, I did," said Charley. "It's for you."

"You'd better hold on to it," said Nancy. She handed the clip back to Charley. "I'll keep the change." And she put the rest of Charley's money in her pocket.

At that moment Charley heard a voice.

"Great Caesar's ghost! It's Charley! How did you get in here?"

Charley looked up and saw his father coming across the room with another man. They pulled up chairs and sat down at Charley's table.

His father said, "If this isn't King Charles himself, it looks like my son, Charley Rivers. Mr. Rand and I came in here to eat and talk business, but first I want to find out what you're doing here."

"I forgot my lunch box," said Charley, and he told his father everything that had happened.

"So one thing led to another, just like yesterday," his father said. "Didn't anyone offer you any lunch at school?"

"Yes," said Charley. "One girl did. But she didn't have a lot to spare."

"So you came here," his father said. "And what did you have to eat?"

Charley told him. "Here's the bill," he said. "I couldn't eat everything they gave me, and it cost a lot."

His father looked at the bill. "It certainly did," he said. "Well, I'll pay the bill, and you can pay me back out of your allowance. It will take you quite a while. That will help you to remember two important things: Don't run up big bills in fancy places. And don't forget your lunch box."

Mr. Rand laughed. "This boy has a great future," he said. "I'm always looking for young fellows who think of new ways to solve problems. Send Charley around to me about ten years from now. I'll give him a job."

"Well!" said Charley's father. "You never know when you wake up in the morning what's going to happen before you go to bed at night." He looked at his watch. "Hadn't you better hurry?" he asked.

"Yes," said Charley. "I don't want to be late twice in one day. Good-by, Mr. Rand, I'll come to see you about that job some day. See you to-night," he said to his father. "Thanks for paying the bill. You'll have a nice waitress if you eat at this table. Her name's Nancy. Mrs. Ruggles is the hostess."

"You've made quite a few friends at the King Charles," his father said.

"It's my favorite hotel," said Charley.

Just then someone stopped on the sidewalk and

pressed his nose against the plate-glass window. It was Wally Williams. His mouth was wide open. "I've got to go," said Charley. He walked quickly through the King Charles dining room, and Mrs. Ruggles helped him put on his coat and cap.

"Good-by, he said. With one hand on the door he turned. "Are you Rosabelle's mother?" he asked.

"Yes, I am," she said, looking surprised. "How did you know?"

"I just guessed," said Charley. He ran out to the big front door.

Mr. Murphy opened it for him. Wally Williams was standing there, waiting. Other boys and girls were going by on their way back to school.

"What were you doing in there?" asked Wally.

"Tell you later," said Charley. "Good-by, Mr. Murphy. Thanks a lot for helping me out. I hope I can do something for you some time. My father's going to pay the bill."

"Good," said Mr. Murphy. "Was your father surprised to see you?"

"Sure was," said Charley. He and Wally hurried off.

"What happened?" asked Wally.

"I forgot my lunch box," said Charley. "I went to the King Charles for lunch."

"You did?" said Wally. "They let you in? All by yourself?"

"Yes," said Charley. "They probably wouldn't have, but Mr. Murphy is a friend of mine."

"What was it like in there?" asked Wally.

"It was great," said Charley. "But I don't think I'll ever go again—not by myself, I mean. It cost too much and the lunch was too big. I'll give you a piece of chocolate cake that I couldn't eat. I met some nice people, though. I met a waitress named Nancy. And say! I met Rosabelle's mother!"

"You did?" said Wally, without much interest.

"Yes," said Charley. "She's the new hostess in the King Charles dining room." Suddenly he had an idea. "I'll bet that's where Rosabelle gets those big lunches!"

"What lunches?" asked Wally.

"Tomato soup, chicken legs, fruit salad, chocolate cake. I'll bet her mother gets them from the kitchen of the King Charles."

"Sure," said Wally. "A lot of food goes to waste in hotel kitchens. If you work there, you can probably get the leftovers at a bargain."

"Maybe you can get them for nothing," said Charley. "From now on I'll know what they had left over at the King Charles."

"Who cares?" said Wally. "I think Rosabelle is kind of dumb. She hasn't said a word to me."

"Me neither," said Charley. "Maybe when she's not so new, she'll say something. Anyway, she's pretty."

"Oh, I don't know," said Wally. "What do you think of Jane Lane?"

Charley remembered how Jane had offered him half of her lunch. Of all the nice things that people had done for him today, that was the nicest.

"Well," he said, "most of the time she's just all

right, but she sure looked great today. I'm going to give her a valentine I bought at the King Charles."

"That reminds me," he went on, "we ought to get going on our bird houses right after school."

"What's the hurry?" asked Wally.

"The sooner we finish the bird houses, the sooner we can start on a shack," said Charley. "I've had another idea, too. When we get to beavers in science class, I'm going to do a special project. Miss Gay will think it's a knockout!"

"When did you get all these ideas?" asked Wally, impressed.

"Yesterday when I was shopping at the King Charles," said Charley.

They reached the school yard. "Everybody else has gone in," said Charley. "We'd better run or we'll be late."

They ran through the school yard. The wind was blowing the swings. They clanged against each other, but it wasn't a lonely sound now.

"Sounds like bells!" said Charley. He and Wally ran into the school, and the door closed behind them.

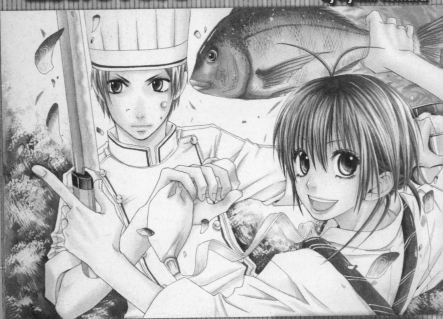

LOVE★COM VOL 11
The Shojo Beat Manga Edition

STORY AND ART BY
AYA NAKAHARA

Translation & English Adaptation/Pookie Rolf
Touch-up Art & Lettering/Gia Cam Luc
Design/Yuki Ameda
Editors/Pancha Diaz & Carrie Shepherd

Editor in Chief, Books/Alvin Lu
Editor in Chief, Magazines/Marc Weidenbaum
VP, Publishing Licensing /Rika Inouye
VP, Sales & Product Marketing/Gonzalo Ferreyra
VP, Creative/Linda Espinosa
Publisher/Hyoe Narita

Printed in Canada

Published by VIZ Media, LLC
P.O. Box 77010
San Francisco, CA 94107

Shojo Beat Manga Edition
10 9 8 7 6 5 4 3 2 1
First printing, March 2009

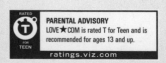

PARENTAL ADVISORY
LOVE★COM is rated T for Teen and is
recommended for ages 13 and up.
ratings.viz.com

store.viz.com

NAKAOCCHI

All the electrical appliances in my apartment are slightly out of whack, and they only work perfectly when the repairman comes over. In other words, they have bad personalities. The TV, in particular. Sometimes when I turn it on, it makes this high-pitched whine. I'm like, if you're going to whine, whine all the time! I mean, the repairman comes over and it puts on this smooth-faced quiet act. And then, after he's gone, it sniggers at me and starts whining again. That stinker!

Aya Nakahara won the 2003 Shogakukan Manga Award for her breakthrough hit *Love★Com*, which was made into a major motion picture and a PS2 game in 2006. She debuted with *Haru to Kuuki Nichiyou-bi* in 1995, and her other works include *HANADA* and *Himitsu Kichi*.

glossary

Page 6, panel 4: Hatsumode
The shrine visit on New Year's Day in Japan. The gang is suggesting going out on New Year's Eve, but visiting the shrine after midnight, when it is technically New Year's Day. Because many people do the same thing, trains often run all night long.

Page 11, panel 3: Chūka-man
The Japanese name for *baozi*, or Chinese buns. Pork-filled buns are called *buta-man*, curry-filled buns are called *curry-man*, etc.

Page 25, panel 5: Takoyaki
Fried octopus balls, a popular festival food.

Page 46, panel 2: Yakitori
Grilled chicken on skewers, also a popular festival food.

Page 52, panel 3: Senbei
Senbei are Japanese rice crackers that are either baked, grilled or fried. These senbei are soy sauce flavored.

Page 58, panel 5: New Year's gift money
In Japan on New Year's, it is traditional to give children money, called *otoshidama*. The money is handed out in small, decorated envelopes sometimes called *pochibukuro*, similar to the envelopes used to hand out money for Chinese New Year.

Page 95, sidebar: Yakisoba
A stir-fried noodle dish similar to chow mein. It is commonly made with pork and various vegetables such as cabbage, carrots and onions. It can also be served on a bun in a kind of sandwich called *yakisoba pan*.

HE'S GOING TO BE JUST FINE. I DON'T NEED TO WORRY ABOUT HIM.

KA-CHAK

HOW'RE WE DOING, MR. ŌTANI?

WOULD YOU CARE FOR A LITTLE LATE-NIGHT SNACK, PERHAPS?

...OH.

♡Bound

BUT HE NEEDS TO GET SOME REST OR HE'LL BE A WRECK TOMORROW.

WOULD HE WANT ME TO WAKE HIM UP?

HE'S ASLEEP.

OKAY, THEN!

STUDY HARD! I'LL SEE YOU LATER.

...OKAY.

College ♥ Bound

KYUP

ALL RIGHT! HERE WE GO!

HYARGH, DARN IT!

THE EXAM!!

WELL, RATHER THAN WORRYING ABOUT MY PARENTS, MAYBE YOU OUGHT TO BE WORRYING ABOUT TOMORROW'S EXAM.

AND YOU NEED TO CONCENTRATE RIGHT NOW.

IF I STAY, I'M GONNA TALK TO YOU. I COULDN'T HELP IT.

YOU'RE GONNA STUDY AS LATE AS YOU CAN, AREN'T YOU?

SO I'LL BE IN MY BROTHER'S ROOM IF YOU NEED ANYTHING.

OH... THANKS. SORRY.

KA-CHAK

COME GET ME IF YOU NEED ANYTHING, OKAY? PROMISE?

YEAH.

...

HUH?

YOU DON'T HAVE TO LEAVE YOUR ROOM.

...SORRY, ŌTANI...

KTONF

SORRY ABOUT THAT. YOU'RE REALLY TIRED, AREN'T YOU?

SLUMP

I MEAN, WHAT THE HECK AM I DOING HERE?! IT'S THE NIGHT BEFORE MY ENTRANCE EXAMS AND I'M...

NO I'M NOT! I'M CRAZY, AREN'T I?!

SSSSH SSSSH SSSSH... OKAAAY, LET'S CALM DOWN...

I'M OKAY...

I KNOW, I'M ONLY FIVE FOOT ONE AND A BIT, AND I'M REALLY SORRY ABOUT THAT, SIR!!

SHORT!!

BUT YOU'RE SO...

OHH...

ŌTANI, AND I'M, UH, D-D-D-DATING Y-Y-YOUR DAUGHTER KOIZUMI, I MEAN, R-R-RISA.

I, UH, MY NAME IS, UH...

UH, NICE, TO UM, M-M-MEET YOU, SIR...

UM!

HEY!!

Not you too, Dad!

THAT'S FINE, I WAS JUST WONDERING IF THIS IS OKAY WITH YOU...

HE'S SPENDING THE NIGHT HERE TONIGHT.

I'M REALLY SORRY ABOUT SHOWING UP LIKE THIS TONIGHT!!

OH, THAT'S OKAY.

YEAH.

WE DON'T HAVE SCHOOL TOMORROW, SO I WAS GONNA SPEND THE NIGHT.

And what can I get you?

YOU'RE OVER AT NOBU'S HOUSE?!

...

YOU WANT ME TO GO HOME?

ASK RISA IF YOU CAN SPEND THE NIGHT AT HER HOUSE.

SUZUKI'S PROBABLY IN FINAL CRUNCH MODE TOO...

Gimme.

I DON'T KNOW...

YOU GUYS DON'T HAVE THAT MUCH TIME LEFT TOGETHER. I'M NOT BUSTING THAT UP.

...NUH-UH.

SO WHERE ARE YOU GONNA GO, THEN?

Huh? **WHAT** ENTRANCE EXAMS?

...

hff

...I'M JUST SO NERVOUS ABOUT THOSE ENTRANCE EXAMS TOMORROW...

MY BOY-FRIEND'S ENTRANCE EXAMS...?

Since you ask?

I WONDER HOW ŌTANI'S DOING.

BET HE'S STUDYING UP TO THE LAST MINUTE...

OH GOSH, I REALLY HOPE HE'S OKAY.

WHAAAT?!

RISA! YOU NEVER SAID ANYTHING ABOUT A BOYFRIEND BEFORE?!

WHAT BOY-FRIEND?!

WHAAAT?!

WELL, I WASN'T KEEPING IT A SECRET OR ANY-THING...

BUT I GUESS THE SUBJECT JUST NEVER CAME UP BEFORE.

CUZ HE IS STRETCHED TO HIS VERY FURTHEST LIMITS, POOR GUY.

COME ON, ŌTANI.

YOU CAN DO IT!

I'M HOME...

KA-CHAK

ŌTANI'S UNIVERSITY ENTRANCE EXAMS...

...ARE TOMORROW.

AND THEN YOU GUYS GET TO INDULGE IN ALL THE HOOCHY-KOOCHY YOU'VE BEEN DEPRIVED OF!

OMIGOSH, *MY* STOMACH'S STARTING TO HURT, I'M SO NERVOUS.

THINK ABOUT IT THIS WAY— AFTER TOMORROW, HE WON'T HAVE TO STUDY ANY-MORE!

HEY, RELAX!

TWINGE TWINGE

137

...

DON'T WORRY, IT'S OKAY... JUST PUSH THE TOP AND MORE LEAD WILL COME OUT.

YOU'RE RIGHT!!

OH WOW, PHEWWW!!

CH*k

...I DON'T THINK SO.

MY STOMACH HURTS. I THINK I HAVE AN ULCER. IT'S KILLING ME.

TWIN*E TWIN*E

...

ARE YOU REALLY GONNA GET THROUGH THIS OKAY...?

...BUT ACTU-ALLY...

...THERE'S SOMEBODY ELSE WHO SHOULD BE GETTING MY UNDIVIDED ATTENTION RIGHT NOW.

CONGRATU-
LATIONS,
NOBU-CHAN.

SHE AND
NAKAO
SEEM TO
BE EVEN
MORE LOVEY-
DOVEY WITH
EACH OTHER
THAN BEFORE.

WHICH IS
REALLY
GREAT.

Wanna
come
over
after
school?

Yeah,
for
sure.

NOBU GOT A LETTER FROM THE JUNIOR COLLEGE IN HOKKAIDO SAYING SHE'D BEEN ACCEPTED AND WOULD BE ENROLLED IN APRIL.

WOW! CON-GRATU-LATIONS!!

NAH, I TOTALLY KNEW I'D PASS. IT WAS A PIECE OF CAKE!

WELL, THAT'S A HUGE LOAD OFF YOUR MIND, HUH?!

CHAPTER 44

I...

...

...I HOPE YOU DO REALLY WELL ON THAT EXAM.

GOOD LUCK, NOBU-CHAN!

Phone call
Risa

117

CHUCKLE

Ma... i...

Migh... ty...

Right?

MY NAME IS MAIKO.

WHAT A FUNNY THING TO SAY!

SMILE

Omigod.

I WANT YOU TO MEET MY BEAUTIFUL MISTRESS, MAIKO.

!

Suzu...

SHUP

WHADDAYA THINK YOU'RE DOING, YA BIG DOPE?!

Take that ugmo wig off, for pete's sake!!

CHUCKLE

SUZUKO!!

OH PLEASE. NOT YOU TOO.

WHADDAYA MEAN, LEAVE YOU ALONE?!

FINE, WHATEVER, JUST LEAVE ME ALONE!!

SORRY ABOUT THAT EARLIER. ♡

I DON'T WANT NOBU TO GO AWAY EITHER.

SO PLEASE, NAKAO. COME ON.

YOU HAVE TO DO IT.

Bzzzz

Saa ya, bye!

BUT IF HER OWN BOY-FRIEND'S BEING SO CON-SIDERATE THAT HE DOESN'T TELL HER TO STAY...

...THEN I SURE CAN'T ASK HER TO.

SH WAP

HEY.

I WISH THERE WAS SOMETHING I COULD DO TO HELP HER, BUT...

...YEAH...

YOU JUST GOTTA LET HER REACH HER OWN DECISION AND BE READY FOR WHATEVER THAT IS.

SO SHE HEARD YOU, TOO BAD. YOU CAN'T DO ANYTHING ABOUT IT NOW, RIGHT?

But the leftovers always get eaten by somebody, okay? We don't throw food away, okay?

So anyway, that's what it's like at my house. Like, I just had some yakisoba. Super-greasy yakisoba. A huge mound of them. Like, excuse me, but this is not a competitive eating event!

Lately I've been eating a lot of Japanese cuisine. And really enjoying it. Even sashimi, which I used to hate so much, is a big favorite now. I guess your tastes change as you grow older.

Waaah...My mom just brought me some cake. I just had yakisoba, remember? You saw me eat it, right? I'm sorry, but there is no way I can have cake right now.

 In that case, allow me to eat it for you.

HE'S RIGHT.

WHO KNOWS WHAT HE'S GONNA FALL OFF OF NEXT? HE COULD GET REALLY HURT...

I MEAN, THE DUDE'S A TOTAL BASKET CASE.

YIKES

I WAS SO WORRIED ABOUT NOBU, BUT ACTUALLY, NAKAO'S IN WAY WORSE SHAPE...

HI! YOU GUYS...

GLOOOOM

WHAT'S THE MATTER WITH *YOU*?

blah

blah

NWARRRRGH...

I JUST WISH... I COULD THINK OF A WAY FOR NOBU TO WORK THIS OUT.

FORGET IT. DON'T EVEN TRY.

IT'S HER LIFE AND YOU BUTTIN' IN ISN'T GONNA HELP.

THE ONE I'M CONCERNED ABOUT, ACTUALLY, IS NAKAO.

I KNOW, BUT STILL...

94

YEAH, BUT YOU CAN'T TELL FROM PICTURES. I ALWAYS WANTED TO VISIT WITH YOU, BUT YOU NEVER TOOK ME.

Cuz it's so far away.

OH, THAT'S RIGHT, YOU'VE NEVER BEEN THERE, HAVE YOU, NOBUKO? WELL, LET ME SEE... I'VE SHOWN YOU PICTURES THOUGH, HAVEN'T I?

WHAT'S IT LIKE THERE IN HOKKAIDO? YOU GREW UP THERE, RIGHT?

BUT THE AIR'S REAL CLEAN AND THE SKY'S REAL HUGE... IT'S A NICE PLACE.

WELL, NOT MUCH TO TELL, REALLY. THERE'S NOTHING THERE.

IT'S REALLY COLD UP THERE, A LOT COLDER 'N OSAKA. SO YOU'LL NEED TO BUY A LOT OF WARM CLOTHES TO TAKE WITH YOU.

UH-HUH.

OH, BUT NOBUKO...

NOBU'S AN ONLY CHILD AND BOTH OF HER PARENTS WORK, SO...

...SHE SPENT ALL HER TIME WITH HER GRANDMA WHEN SHE WAS LITTLE, SHE TOLD ME.

SHE SAID MY PARENTS GAVE ME A HEALTHY, PERFECT BODY AND I SHOULDN'T MUTILATE IT.

I KINDA THINK SHE'S RIGHT. SO I'M LEAVING MY EARS ALONE.

AAA-HHH...

HEY, GRANDMA?

YOU LIKE THAT?

THAT FEELS *SOOO* GOOD, NOBUKO.

EVEN THOUGH NOBU REALLY LOVES FASHION AND JEWELRY...

...ONE THING SHE WON'T DO IS GET HER EARS PIERCED.

OOH, THESE EARRINGS ARE SOOO CUUUTE.

WISH I COULD WEAR THEM.

MY GRANDMA GOT REALLY MAD AND TOTALLY CHEWED ME OUT.

ONLY I MESSED IT UP AND GOT BLOOD ALL OVER THE PLACE.

I PIERCED MY EARS BY MYSELF, BACK IN JUNIOR HIGH, WITH A NEEDLE AND ICE CUBES.

CHAPTER 43

COME ON, NAKAO, WE'RE GOING.

...TO BE SEPARATED FROM NOBU-CHAN EITHER.

I DON'T WANT...

ME EEEEEE-EITHER-RRRR...

I DON'T GET WHAT YOU'RE TALKING ABOOOO-OUT...

SHE MUST'VE BEEN REALLY, REALLY TORN. BUT AFTER THINKING REALLY LONG AND HARD ABOUT IT...

WHO'D WANT TO LEAVE THEIR BOYFRIEND BEHIND AND GO FAR AWAY?

...SHE DECIDED TO GO.

NOBODY, OBVIOUSLY. LIKE, DUH.

HOW COME YOU'RE CRYING, RISA?

WELL, GOSH...

HUH?

DOES IT SEEM LIKE I'M OUT OF IT?

NO, YOU SEEMED LIKE YOU WERE *TOTALLY IN CONTROL* AS YOU *FELL DOWN THE STAIRS!!*

OHH... YEAH.

YEAH, I GUESS THAT WASN'T TOO TOGETHER...

...

ARE YOU *JOKING?!* YOU'VE BEEN A *TOTAL...*

I THOUGHT I'VE BEEN ACTING PRETTY MUCH THE WAY I ALWAYS DO.

...I HAVE...?

YOU'VE BEEN ACTING SUPER-WEIRD LATELY.

...WHAT'S UP WITH YOU?

? WHAT'S THE MATTER, NOBU?

...WELL...

YOU GO AFTER HIM!

I'LL GO TALK TO NOBU SO SHE DOESN'T FIND OUT!

UH... OKAY.

IT'S JUST...

...THAT BABY'S ACTING KINDA FUNNY...

WHO ARE YOU?

HOW'S IT GOING, YOU TWO?!

YOO-HOO, GIRLS!!

ARE WE STUDYING HARD?!

WHUMP

YOU THINK THAT'S BE-CAUSE...

!

HE'S BEEN SPACING OUT SOME-TIMES IN THE WEIRDEST WAY...

HE IS SERIOUSLY LOSING IT.

GIRLS CHANGING ROOM

KA-CHAK

OH, WOW, YEAHHH... THAT'S REALLY NEAT...

NAKAO! YOUR MILK! IT'S SQUIRT-ING OUT!

HUH?!

SKWIRT

USA MILK

WHUMP

THE CLOSER WE GET TO NOBU'S ENTRANCE EXAMS...

...THE MORE NAKAO SEEMS TO BE FALLING APART.

KYAAA

SLAM

WRONG DOOR!!

ARE YOU DOING THIS ON PURPOSE?!

PLUS, HOW COME SHE'S SO CHIRPY, ANYWAY...?

THAT YOU HAD TO HEAR ABOUT ME GOING TO HOKKAIDO FROM KONG.

HUH? ABOUT WHAT?

HEY, I'M SORRY, RISA.

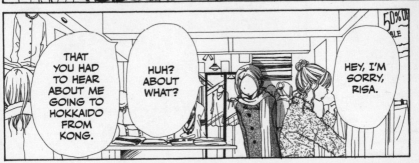

WELL, I GOTTA WHILE I CAN. THEY MIGHT NOT HAVE CUTE STUFF WHERE I'M GOING. IT'S THE TOTAL BOONIES.

ARE YOU REALLY GOING TO BUY ALL OF THOSE?

OH. THAT'S OKAY. YOU JUST DECIDED IT, RIGHT?

YEAH, I DID.

PLUS I GOT A LOT OF NEW YEAR'S GIFT MONEY FROM MY GRANDMA!

OHH YEAH, THAT'S RIGHT.

②🐰

Writing something serious for a change has made me hungry. I'm a small eater though, so I can never put away much. The single portions of this world are too big, if you ask me. Don't you think? My mom always makes a ton of food when she cooks, saying, "If you can't eat it, just leave it," so I guess my habit of leaving things on my plate comes from that too. Shame on me! Even now I live real close to my parents' house, so my mom comes over to cook for me, which is very nice of her, but you wouldn't believe what she makes.

Dinner one evening

Ramen

Super-greasy "shiny fried rice" (a signature dish)

Meat

And then, imagine hearing, "I'm just frying up some breaded prawns for you." I mean, my god, this is a meal that you get full just looking at. Plus, the prawns come with the heads attached. They're huge. This is what she considers one person's portion. Spare me, please...

HOW COULD NOBU DECIDE TO GO SO FAR AWAY FOR SO LONG?

I JUST DON'T GET IT.

BZZZz

WANNA GO SHOPPING AFTER SCHOOL TODAY?

HEY, RISA!

I STUDIED MY BUTT OFF DURING VACATION!

DON'T YOU NEED TO STUDY FOR YOUR ENTRANCE EXAM...?

OKAY...

THE NEW YEAR SALES! IT'S BARGAIN CITY DOWNTOWN!

KOI-
ZUMI...

I MEAN, JUST TALKING ON THE PHONE?

I COULDN'T STAND IT, I JUST COULDN'T.

LIVING FAR AWAY FROM YOU? FOR A FEW *YEARS...?*

HEY! LIKE I'M A MUNCHKIN OR SOME-THING!!

IT'S NOT THE SAME. I NEED TO SEE YOU IN PERSON. I NEED TO LOOK DOWN AT THE TOP OF YOUR HEAD AND TALK TO YOU THAT WAY.

HOW COULD SHE DO IT?

YOU *SAID,* "THE *TOP* OF MY *HEAD"!!*

NO, I MEANT, I NEED TO TALK TO YOU FACE-TO-FACE.

I DON'T KNOW HOW THAT'S GOING TO WORK OUT.

...YEAH...

THOSE TWO ARE NUTS ABOUT EACH OTHER.

IT OUGHT TO BE OKAY. I MEAN, COME ON...

HOW CAN SHE DO IT?! I COULD *NEVER* GO OFF ALONE LIKE THAT!

HUH?

I MEAN, MY GOSH...

HOW?!

HOW WHAT ?!

BUT STILL...

55

MY GRANDMA'S IN KINDA BAD SHAPE, AND SHE'S GOING UP TO HOKKAIDO TO RECUPERATE OUT IN THE COUNTRYSIDE.

SO I THOUGHT I'D GO UP THERE TO BE WITH HER.

BOTH OF THEM WORK, SO THEY CAN'T JUST QUIT THEIR JOBS AND MOVE UP THERE.

I'M THE ONLY ONE WHO CAN.

BUT...

WHAT ABOUT YOUR MOM AND DAD?

...

SO OKAY, SHE USED TO LIVE THERE A LONG TIME AGO AND STILL KNOWS SOME PEOPLE, BUT COME ON. SHE'LL BE REALLY LONELY UP THERE ALL ALONE.

YOU GUYS WANT SOME?

Senbei

IT'S THE LAST TERM OF OUR LAST YEAR IN HIGH SCHOOL...

WELL, WHAT DO YOU WANT TO BE?

I GUESS I'M ABOUT THE ONLY ONE WHO HASN'T DECIDED WHAT TO DO WITH MYSELF STARTING IN APRIL.

Errrr-rmmm...

CHAPTER 42

...THAT IF YOU TOOK OUR FEELINGS FOR EACH OTHER AND WEIGHED THEM...

...WHAT?

...MINE WOULD SEND THE NEEDLE STRAIGHT OFF THE DIAL, BUT HIS WOULDN'T EVEN COME CLOSE.

blah

blah

blah

NOW, THOUGH ...

blah

I'D ALWAYS THOUGHT ...

NOTHING.

DOES ŌTANI EVER FEEL RULED BY THE THINGS I SAY AND DO?

BZZZZ

THAT REALLY PISSES ME OFF!!

...ALL RIGHT, ALL RIGHT.

NO YOU COULDN'T, CUZ I HAD THREE MORE THAN YOU.

OH-KAY!

YOU STAY RIGHT THERE.

COME ONNN, ŌTANI, I'M WAAAIT-ING...I WANT MY TAKOYAKI...

DARRRN...

IF YOU HADN'T SMACKED ME AND MADE ME LOSE THAT ONE GOLDFISH, I COULD'VE...

YIKES

YO!

WORD ON DA STREET! YOU GOT A PHONE CALL!

HANG ON!

WE MANAGED TO GET BACK TOGETHER, SO LET'S GET ALONG TO GREET THE NEW YEAR.

OH WELL.

TOO BAD!

AAAAGH!! I SCOOPED THAT ONE!!

HEY, CHECK IT OUT! I GOT TWO AT THE SAME TIME!

WHICH IS TOTALLY UNFAIR.

IT ALWAYS SEEMS LIKE *I'M* RULED BY *HIM*, NEVER THE OTHER WAY AROUND.

THAT REALLY PISSES ME OFF! I AM GOING TO WIN THIS NO MATTER WHAT!!

I WIN.

WELL SO AM I, SO THERE!!

① 🐰

Hello, Nakahara here.

How are you all doing?

So...we're up to volume 11. That's getting up there to the number of volumes you want to sell off as one big collection. I mean, 11 volumes. That takes up a lot of shelf space!

I had past volumes lined up at the back of my desk for checking stuff while working, but I can't fit them all there anymore!! Well, I'm a very fortunate person indeed. I've never had the occasion to work on the same title for such a loooooong time before. So each episode's a new challenge for me. It's really, really scary while at the same time fun because of the discoveries I get to make. So I'm learning something with every episode. But there's so much more that I want to learn.

As a matter of fact, I happen to love studying. I'm having a lot of fun studying these days. What's the subject? How to make people laugh.

OH WOW, HARUKA! I HAVEN'T SEEN YOU IN A WHILE!

RISA!

DON'T WORRY, SENPAI! I'M GOING TO KEEP A TIGHT HOLD ON HIM...

WARGH!!

...SO HE DOESN'T GO BUSTING IN BETWEEN YOU AND ŌTANI SENPAI AND BEING A TOTAL PEST.

THANK YOU.

Hee hee

CON-GRATU-LATIONS.

I'M SO GLAD FOR YOU, RISA!

I HEARD YOU AND ŌTANI MADE UP AND GOT BACK TOGETHER.

Whaddaya mean, "Thank You"?! Risa!!

HOPE HE'S GONNA BE OKAY...

BUT...

My hat.

What's that on your head?

I'm back from my break.

pot

...ŌTANI MIGHT NOT HAVE COME LOOKING FOR ME IF KOHORI-KUN HADN'T BEEN THERE.

...CHRIST-MAS EVE...

Oops, I made a mistake. Here's my hat.

THANK YOU, KOHORI-KUN. AND SORRY.

OOPS.

I'D TOTALLY FORGOTTEN ABOUT...

OH, HI...

GLOOOOM

...YOU SURE SEEM TO BE IN A GOOD MOOD, KOIZUMI-SAN...

BA-ZONK

HUH...?

UH, YEAH...

...

KOHORI-KUN. HOW'S IT GOING...?

IT'S OKAY... YOU DON'T HAVE TO SAY ANYTHING...

KLUNK

...I THOUGHT YOU MIGHT'VE...

UMM...

DID YOU MAYBE GET BACK TOGETHER WITH YOUR BOYFRIEND OR SOMETHING...?

16

HE CAN TAKE ONE NIGHT OFF.

OH, BUT... CAN ŌTANI EVEN GO? HE MIGHT BE STUDYING.

AND THEN WE CAN ALL DO THE NEW YEAR'S EVE COUNTDOWN TOGETHER.

LET US SEE YOU GUYS HOLDING HANDS, AT LEAST.

OOH, THAT SOUNDS LIKE A LOT OF FUN!

WINTER BREAK STARTED, THEN CHRISTMAS CAME AND WENT...

IS IT OKAY?!

Yaaay♡

WANNA COME TOO, SEIKO-CHAN?

...

We'd love to have you come.

...AND NEXT THING I KNOW, IT'S NEW YEAR'S EVE.

OKAY, SO I'LL CALL CHIHARU ABOUT IT TOO.

I GUESS IT WON'T HURT TO ASK HIM ANYWAY.

WAIT A SEC...

MORE THAN HE THOUGHT ...?

IT TURNS OUT I LOVE YOU MORE THAN I THOUGHT.

SO HOW MUCH DID HE THINK HE LOVED ME BEFORE?

OHH, AFTER ALL THAT STUFF ABOUT BREAKING UP?

CHAPTER 41

love ☆ com

11

A HAPPY
NEW YEAR

Story & Art by
Aya Nakahara

love ★ com

contents 11

The Story So Far...

Risa and Ôtani are their class's lopsided comedy duo...except that Risa falls in love with Ôtani! She finally works up the courage to tell him how she feels, only to be rejected. Even so, she keeps trying to change his mind, and finally they start going out...but will they stay together?! It's looking dicey...because Ôtani wants to go to college and Risa doesn't. So he's studying his butt off for the entrance exams, while Risa has taken a waitressing job. Not only do they hardly ever see each other anymore, but Kohori, a cute guy at work, has a huge crush on Risa...and after Ôtani catches him kissing her while she's asleep, he runs into Risa and Kohori out together. That's it! Ôtani breaks up with Risa!! But not for long...

♥ To really get all the details, check out Lovely Complex Vol. 1-10, available at bookstores everywhere!!

Shojo Beat

love ★ com

11

Story & Art by
Aya Nakahara